Sir Arthur Conan Doyle

Songs of Action

Sir Arthur Conan Doyle

Songs of Action

ISBN/EAN: 9783744766937

Printed in Europe, USA, Canada, Australia, Japan

Cover: Foto ©Andreas Hilbeck / pixelio.**de**

More available books at **www.hansebooks.com**

SONGS OF ACTION

BY

A. CONAN DOYLE

AUTHOR OF "MICAH CLARKE," "THE WHITE COMPANY,"
"RODNEY STONE," "UNCLE BERNAC," ETC.

NEW YORK
DOUBLEDAY & McCLURE CO.
1898

CONTENTS

SONGS OF ACTION

THE SONG OF THE BOW

What of the bow?
  The bow was made in England:
Of true wood, of yew-wood,
  The wood of English bows;
    So men who are free
    Love the old yew-tree
And the land where the yew-tree grows.

What of the cord?
  The cord was made in England:
A rough cord, a tough cord,
  A cord that bowmen love;

And so we will sing
Of the hempen string
And the land where the cord was wove.

What of the shaft?
The shaft was cut in England:
A long shaft, a strong shaft,
   Barbed and trim and true;
      So we 'll drink all together
      To the gray goose-feather
And the land where the gray goose flew.

What of the mark?
Ah, seek it not in England:
A bold mark, our old mark,
   Is waiting over-sea.
      When the strings harp in chorus,
      And the lion flag is o'er us,
It is there that our mark will be.

What of the men?

The men were bred in England:

The bowmen — the yeomen,

The lads of dale and fell.

Here 's to you — and to you!

To the hearts that are true

And the land where the true hearts dwell.

CREMONA

[The French Army, including a part of the Irish Brigade, under Marshal Villeroy, held the fortified town of Cremona during the winter of 1702. Prince Eugène, with the Imperial Army, surprised it one morning, and, owing to the treachery of a priest, occupied the whole city before the alarm was given. Villeroy was captured, together with many of the French garrison. The Irish, however, consisting of the regiments of Dillon and of Burke, held a fort commanding the river gate, and defended themselves all day, in spite of Prince Eugène's efforts to win them over to his cause. Eventually Eugène, being unable to take the post, was compelled to withdraw from the city.]

The Grenadiers of Austria are proper men
and tall;
The Grenadiers of Austria have scaled the
city wall;

They have marched from far away
Ere the dawning of the day,
And the morning saw them masters of
    Cremona.

There 's not a man to whisper, there 's not
    a horse to neigh,
Of the footmen of Lorraine and the riders
    of Duprés ;
    They have crept up every street,
    In the market-place they meet,
They are holding every vantage in Cre-
    mona.

The Marshal Villeroy he has started from
    his bed;
The Marshal Villeroy has no wig upon
    his head;

"I have lost my men!" quoth he,
"And my men they have lost me,
And I sorely fear we both have lost Cre-
mona."

Prince Eugène of Austria is in the market-
place;
Prince Eugène of Austria has smiles upon
his face;
Says he, "Our work is done,
For the Citadel is won,
And the black and yellow flag flies o'er
Cremona."

Major Dan O'Mahony is in the barrack
square,
And just six hundred Irish lads are waiting for him there;

Says he, " Come in your shirt,
And you won't take any hurt,
For the morning air is pleasant in Cre-
mona."

Major Dan O'Mahony is at the barrack
gate,
And just six hundred Irish lads will nei-
ther stay nor wait;
There 's Dillon and there 's Burke,
And there 'll be some bloody work
Ere the Kaiserlics shall boast they hold
Cremona.

Major Dan O'Mahony has reached the
river fort,
And just six hundred Irish lads are join-
ing in the sport;

"Come, take a hand!" says he,
"And if you will stand by me,
Then it 's glory to the man who takes
Cremona!"

Prince Eugène of Austria has frowns upon
his face,
And loud he calls his Galloper of Irish
blood and race :
"MacDonnell, ride, I pray,
To your countrymen, and say
That only they are left in all Cremona!"

MacDonnell he has reined his mare beside
the river dike,
And he has tied the parley flag upon a
sergeant's pike ;
Six companies were there
From Limerick and Clare,
The last of all the guardians of Cremona.

"Now, Major Dan O'Mahony, give up the
river gate,
Or, Major Dan O'Mahony, you 'll find it is
too late;
For when I gallop back
'T is the signal for attack,
And no quarter for the Irish in Cremona¹"

And Major Dan he laughed: "Faith, if
what you say be true,
And if they will not come until they hear
again from you,
Then there will be no attack,
For you 're never going back,
And we 'll keep you snug and safely in
Cremona."

All the weary day the German stormers
came,
All the weary day they were faced by fire
and flame;

They have filled the ditch with
    dead,
And the river 's running red,
But they cannot win the gateway of
    Cremona.

All the weary day, again, again, again,
The horsemen of Duprés and the footmen
    of Lorraine,
    Taafe and Herberstein,
    And the riders of the Rhine;
It 's a mighty price they 're paying for
    Cremona.

Time and time they came with the deep-
    mouthed German roar,
Time and time they broke like the wave
    upon the shore;

For better men were there
From Limerick and Clare,
And who will take the gateway of Cre-
mona?

Prince Eugène has watched, and he gnaws
his nether lip;
Prince Eugène has cursed as he saw his
chances slip:
"Call off! Call off!" he cried,
" It is nearing eventide,
And I fear our work is finished in
Cremona."

Says Wauchop to McAulliffe, " Their
fire is growing slack."
Says Major Dan O'Mahony, " It is their
last attack;

But who will stop the game
While there 's light to play the same,
And to walk a short way with them from
Cremona ? "

And so they snarl behind them, and beg
them turn and come,
They have taken Neuberg's standard, they
have taken Diak's drum ;
And along the winding Po,
Beard on shoulder, stern and slow
The Kaiserlics are riding from Cremona.

Just two hundred Irish lads are shouting
on the wall ;
Four hundred more are lying who can
hear no slogan call ;
But what 's the odds of that,
For it 's all the same to Pat
If he pays his debt in Dublin or Cremona.

Says General de Vaudray, " You 've done
    a soldier's work !
And every tongue in France shall talk of
    Dillon and of Burke !
    Ask what you will this day,
    And be it what it may,
It is granted to the heroes of Cremona."

" Why, then," says Dan O'Mahony, " one
    favor we entreat,
We were called a little early, and our
    toilet 's not complete.
    We 've no quarrel with the shirt,
    But the breeches would n't hurt,
For the evening air is chilly in Cremona."

THE STORMING PARTY

Said Paul Leroy to Barrow,
" Though the breach is steep and narrow,
   If we only gain the summit
      Then it 's odds we hold the fort.
I have ten and you have twenty,
And the thirty should be plenty,
With Henderson and Henty
      And McDermott in support."

Said Barrow to Leroy,
" It 's a solid job, my boy,
   For they 've flanked it, and they 've
      banked it,
      And they 've bored it with a mine.

But it 's only fifty paces
Ere we look them in the faces;
And the men are in their places,
    With their toes upon the line."

Said Paul Leroy to Barrow,
" See that first ray, like an arrow,
   How it tinges all the fringes
    Of the sullen drifting skies.
They told me to begin it
At five-thirty to the minute,
And at thirty-one I 'm in it,
    Or my sub will get his rise.

" So we 'll wait the signal rocket,
Till . . . Barrow, show that locket,
That turquoise-studded locket,
Which you slipped from out your pocket
    And are pressing with a kiss!

Turquoise-studded, spiral-twisted,
It is hers! And I had missed it
From her chain; and you have kissed it:
    Barrow, villain, what is this?"

" Leroy, I had a warning,
That my time has come this morning,
So I speak with frankness, scorning
    To deny the thing that 's true.
Yes, it 's Amy's, is the trinket,
Little turquoise-studded trinket,
Not her gift — oh, never think it!
    For her thoughts were all for you.

" As we danced I gently drew it
From her chain — she never knew it;
But I love her — yes, I love her:
    I am candid, I confess.

But I never told her, never,
For I knew 't was vain endeavor,
And she loved you—loved you ever,
    Would to God she loved you less!"

"Barrow, Barrow, you shall pay me!
Me, your comrade, to betray me!
Well I know that little Amy
    Is as true as wife can be.
She to give this love-badged locket!
She had rather . . . Ha, the rocket!
Hi, McDougall!   Sound the bugle!
    Yorkshires, Yorkshires, follow me!"

    .   .   .   .   .   .

Said Paul Leroy to Amy,
" Well, wifie, you may blame me,
For my passion overcame me,
    When he told me of his shame.

But when I saw him lying,
Dead amid a ring of dying,
Why, poor devil, I was trying
    To forget and not to blame.

"And this locket, I unclasped it
From the fingers that still grasped it;
He told me how he got it,
    How he stole it in a valse."
And she listened leaden-hearted:
Oh, the weary day they parted!
For she loved him—yes, she loved him—
For his youth and for his truth,
    And for those dying words, so false.

THE FRONTIER LINE

What marks the frontier line?
  Thou man of India, say!
Is it the Himalayas sheer,
The rocks and valleys of Cashmere,
Or Indus as she seeks the south
From Attoch to the fivefold mouth?
  "Not that! Not that!"
  Then answer me, I pray!
What marks the frontier line?

What marks the frontier line?
  Thou man of Burma, speak!
Is it traced from Mandalay,
And down the marches of Cathay,

From Bhamo south to Kiang-mai,
And where the buried rubies lie?
"Not that! Not that!"
Then tell me what I seek :
What marks the frontier line?

What marks the frontier line?
Thou Africander, say!
Is it shown by Zulu kraal,
By Drakensberg or winding Vaal,
Or where the Shiré waters seek
Their outlet east at Mozambique?
"Not that! Not that!
There is a surer way
To mark the frontier line."

What marks the frontier line?
Thou man of Egypt, tell!
Is it traced on Luxor's sand,
Where Karnak's painted pillars stand,

Or where the river runs between
The Ethiop and Bishareen?
   "Not that! Not that!
   By neither stream nor well
We mark the frontier line.

" But be it east or west,
   One common sign we bear,
The tongue may change, the soil, the sky,
But where your British brothers lie,
The lonely cairn, the nameless grave,
Still fringe the flowing Saxon wave.
      'T is that! 'T is where
   They lie—the men who placed it there,
That marks the frontier line."

CORPORAL DICK'S PROMOTION

A BALLAD OF '82

The Eastern day was well-nigh o'er
When, parched with thirst and travel sore,
Two of McPherson's flanking corps
 Across the Desert were tramping.
They had wandered off from the beaten
 track
And now were wearily harking back,
Ever staring round for the signal jack
 That marked their comrades camping.

The one was Corporal Robert Dick,
Bearded and burly, short and thick,
Rough of speech and in temper quick,
 A hard-faced old rapscallion.

The other, fresh from the barrack square,
Was a raw recruit, smooth-cheeked and
    fair,
Half grown, half drilled, with the weedy air
    Of a draft from the home battalion.

Weary and parched and hunger-torn,
They had wandered on from early morn,
And the young boy-soldier limped forlorn,
    Now stumbling and now falling.
Around the orange sand-curves lay,
Flecked with boulders, black or gray,
Death-silent, save that far away
    A kite was shrilly calling.

A kite? Was *that* a kite? The yell
That shrilly rose and faintly fell?
No kite's, and yet the kite knows well
    The long-drawn, wild halloo.

And right athwart the evening sky
The yellow sand-spray spurtled high,
And shrill and shriller swelled the cry
    Of " Allah ! Allahu ! "

The Corporal peered at the crimson West,
Hid his pipe in his khaki vest.
Growled out an oath and onward pressed,
    Still glancing over his shoulder.
" Bedouins, mate ! " he curtly said;
" We 'll find some work for steel and lead,
" And maybe sleep in a sandy bed,
    Before we 're one hour older.

" But just one flutter before we 're done.
Stiffen your lip and stand, my son ;
We 'll take this bloomin' circus on :
    Ball-cartridge load ! Now, steady ! "

With a curse and a prayer the two faced
    round,
Dogged and grim they stood their ground,
And their breech-blocks snapped with a
    crisp clean sound
      As the rifles sprang to the "ready."

Alas for the Emir Ali Khan!
A hundred paces before his clan,
That ebony steed of the prophet's breed
      Is the foal of death and of danger.
A spurt of fire, a gasp of pain,
A bluish blur on the yellow plain,
The chief was down, and his bridle rein
      Was in the grip of the stranger.

With the light of hope on his rugged face,
The Corporal sprang to the dead man's
    place,

One prick with the steel, one thrust with
   the heel,
     And where was the man to outride
     him?
A grip of his knees, a toss of his rein,
He was settling her down to her gallop
   again,
When he stopped, for he heard just one
   faltering word
     From the young recruit beside him.

One faltering word from pal to pal,
But it found the heart of the Corporal.
He had sprung to the sand, he had lent
   him a hand,
     " Up, mate! They 'll be 'ere in a
     minute;
Off with you! No palaver! Go!
I 'll bide be'ind and run this show.

Promotion has been cursed slow,
    And this is my chance to win it."

Into the saddle he thrust him quick,
Spurred the black mare with a bayonet
    prick,
Watched her gallop with plunge and with
    kick,
    Away o'er the desert careering.
Then he turned with a softened face,
And loosened the strap of his cartridge-
    case,
While his thoughts flew back to the dear
    old place
    In the sunny Hampshire clearing.

The young boy-private, glancing back,
Saw the Bedouins' wild attack,
And heard the sharp Martini crack.

But as he gazed, already
The fierce fanatic Arab band
Was closing in on every hand,
Until one tawny swirl of sand
    Concealed them in its eddy.

.   .   .   .   .   .

A squadron of British horse that night,
Galloping hard in the shadowy light,
Came on the scene of that last stern fight,
    And found the Corporal lying
Silent and grim on the trampled sand,
His rifle grasped in his stiffened hand,
With the warrior pride of one who died
    'Mid a ring of the dead and the
        dying.

And still when twilight shadows fall,
After the evening bugle-call,
In bivouac or in barrack hall,

His comrades speak of the Corporal,
  His death and his devotion.
And there are some who like to say
That perhaps a hidden meaning lay
In the words he spoke, and that the day
When his rough bold spirit passed away
  Was the day that he won promotion.

A FORGOTTEN TALE

[The scene of this ancient fight, recorded by Frois-
sart, is still called "Altura de los Inglesos." Five
hundred years later Wellington's soldiers were fighting on the same ground.]

"Say, what saw you on the hill,
Campesino Garcia?"
"I saw my brindled heifer there,
A trail of bowmen, spent and bare,
And a little man on a sorrel mare
Riding slow before them."

"Say, what saw you in the vale,
Campesino Garcia?"
"There I saw my lambing ewe
And an army riding through;
Thick and brave the pennons flew
From the lances o'er them."

" Then what saw you on the hill,
    Campesino Garcia ? "
" I saw beside the milking byre,
White with want and black with mire,
The little man with eyes afire
    Marshaling his bowmen."

" Then what saw you in the vale,
    Campesino Garcia ? "
" There I saw my bullocks twain,
And amid my uncut grain
All the hardy men of Spain
    Spurring for their foemen."

" Nay, but there is more to tell,
    Campesino Garcia ! "
" I could not bide the end to view;
I had graver things to do,
Tending on the lambing ewe
    Down among the clover."

" Ah, but tell me what you heard,
    Campesino Garcia ! "
" Shouting from the mountain-side,
Shouting until eventide ;
But it dwindled and it died
    Ere milking time was over."

" Nay, but saw you nothing more,
    Campesino Garcia ? "
" Yes, I saw them lying there,
The little man and sorrel mare ;
And in their ranks the bowmen fair,
    With their staves before them."

" And the hardy men of Spain,
    Campesino Garcia ? "
" Hush ! but we are Spanish too ;
More I may not say to you :
May God's benison, like dew,
    Gently settle o'er them."

PENNARBY MINE

Pennarby shaft is dark and steep,
Eight foot wide, eight hundred deep.
Stout the bucket and tough the cord,
Strong as the arm of Winchman Ford.
    "Never look down!
    Stick to the line!"
That was the saying at Pennarby mine.

A stranger came to Pennarby shaft —
Lord, to see how the miners laughed!
White in the collar and stiff in the hat,
With his patent boots and his silk cravat,
    Picking his way,
    Dainty and fine,
Stepping on tiptoe to Pennarby mine.

Touring from London, so he said.

Was it copper they dug for? or gold?
    or lead?

Where did they find it? How did it
    come?

If he tried with a shovel might *he* get
    some?

    Stooping so much

    Was bad for the spine;

And was n't it warmish in Pennarby mine?

'T was like two worlds that met that day —

The world of work and the world of play;

And the grimy lads from the reeking shaft

Nudged each other and grinned and chaffed.

    "Got 'em all out!"

    "A cousin of mine!"

So ran the banter at Pennarby mine.

And Carnbrae Bob, the Pennarby wit,

Told him the facts about the pit:

How they bored the shaft till the brim-
    stone smell

Warned them off from tapping — well,

    He would n't say what,

    But they took it as sign

To dig no deeper in Pennarby mine.

Then leaning over and peering in,

He was pointing out what he said was tin

In the ten-foot lode — a crash! a jar!

A grasping hand and a splintered bar.

    Gone in his strength,

    With the lips that laughed —

Oh, the pale faces round Pennarby shaft!

Far down on a narrow ledge,

They saw him cling to the crumbling edge.

"Wait for the bucket! Hi, man! Stay!
That rope ain't safe! It 's worn away!
    He 's taking his chance,
    Slack out the line!
Sweet Lord be with him!" cried Pennarby
    mine.

"He 's got him! He has him! Pull with
    a will!
Thank God! He 's over and breathing
    still.
And he—Lord's sakes now! What 's
    that? Well!
Blowed if it ain't our London swell.
    Your heart is right
    If your coat *is* fine:
Give us your hand!" cried Pennarby
    mine.

A ROVER CHANTY

A trader sailed from Stepney town—
Wake her up! Shake her up! Try her
with the mainsail!
A trader sailed from Stepney town
With a keg full of gold and a velvet
gown:
Ho, the bully rover Jack,
Waiting with his yard aback,
Out upon the Lowland sea!

The trader he had a daughter fair—
Wake her up! Shake her up! Try her
with the foresail!
The trader he had a daughter fair,
She had gold in her ears, and gold in her
hair:

All for bully rover Jack,
Waiting with his yard aback,
Out upon the Lowland sea!

"Alas the day, oh daughter mine!—
Shake her up! Wake her up! Try her
    with the topsail!
"Alas the day, oh daughter mine!
Yon red, red flag is a fearsome sign!"
    Ho, the bully rover Jack,
    Reaching on the weather tack,
Out upon the Lowland sea!

"A fearsome flag!" the maiden cried—
Wake her up! Shake her up! Try her
    with the jib-sail!
"A fearsome flag!" the maiden cried,
"But comelier men I never have spied!"

Ho, the bully rover Jack,
Reaching on the weather tack,
Out upon the Lowland sea!

There 's a wooden path that the rovers
know —
Wake her up! Shake her up! Try her
with the headsails!
There 's a wooden path that the rovers
know,
Where none come back, though many
must go:
Ho, the bully rover Jack,
Lying with his yard aback,
Out upon the Lowland sea!

Where is the trader of Stepney town? —
Wake her up! Shake her up! Every
stick a-bending!

Where is the trader of Stepney town?
There 's gold on the capstan, and blood
    on the gown:
    Ho for bully Rover Jack,
    Waiting with his yard aback,
Out upon the Lowland sea!

Where is the maiden who knelt at his
    side? —
Wake her up! Shake her up! Every
    stitch a-drawing!
Where is the maiden who knelt at his
    side?
We gowned her in scarlet, and chose her
    our bride:
    Ho, the bully rover Jack,
    Reaching on the weather tack,
Right across the Lowland sea!

So it's up and it's over to Stornoway Bay,
Pack it on! Crack it on! Try her with
    the stunsails!
It's off on a bowline to Stornoway Bay,
Where the liquor is good and the lasses
    are gay:
    Waiting for their bully Jack,
    Watching for him sailing back,
Right across the Lowland sea.

A BALLAD OF THE RANKS

Who carries the gun?
A lad from over the Tweed.
Then let him go, for well we know
He comes of a soldier breed.
So drink together to rock and heather,
Out where the red deer run,
And stand aside for Scotland's pride—
The man that carries the gun!
For the Colonel rides before,
The Major 's on the flank,
The Captains and the Adjutant
Are in the foremost rank.

But when it 's " Action front ! "
   And fighting 's to be done,
Come one, come all, you stand or fall
   By the man who holds the gun.

Who carries the gun ?
   A lad from a Yorkshire dale.
Then let him go, for well we know
   The heart that never will fail.
Here 's to the fire of Lancashire,
   And here 's to her soldier son !
For the hard-bit north has sent him forth —
   The lad that carries the gun.

Who carries the gun ?
   A lad from a Midland shire.
Then let him go, for well we know
   He comes of an English sire.

Here 's a glass to a Midland lass,
    And each can choose the one,
But east and west we claim the best
    For the man that carries the gun.

Who carries the gun?
    A lad from the hills of Wales.
Then let him go, for well we know
    That Taffy is hard as nails.
There are several ll's in the place where
        he dwells,
    And of w's more than one,
With a Llan and a pen, but it breeds good
        men,
    And it 's they who carry the gun.

Who carries the gun?
    A lad from the windy west.

Then let him go, for well we know
    That he is one of the best.
There 's Bristol rough, and Gloucester
      tough,
    And Devon yields to none.
Or you may get in Somerset
    Your lad to carry the gun.

Who carries the gun?
    A lad from London town.
Then let him go, for well we know
    The stuff that never backs down.
He has learned to joke at the powder
      smoke,
    For he is the fogsmoke's son,
And his heart is light and his pluck is
      right —
    The man who carries the gun.

Who carries the gun?
A lad from the Emerald Isle.
Then let him go, for well we know,
We 've tried him many a while.
We 've tried him east, we 've tried him
west,
We 've tried him sea and land,
But the man to beat old Erin's best
Has never yet been planned.

Who carries the gun?
It 's you, and you, and you;
So let us go, and we won't say no
If they give us a job to do.
Here we stand with a cross-linked hand,
Comrades every one;
So one last cup, and drink it up
To the man who carries the gun!

For the Colonel rides before,
The Major 's on the flank,
The Captains and the Adjutant
Are in the foremost rank.

And when it 's " Action front ! "
And there 's fighting to be done,
Come one, come all, you stand or fall
By the man who holds the gun.

A LAY OF THE LINKS

It 's up and away from our work to-day,
    For the breeze sweeps over the down ;
And it 's hey for a game where the gorse
    blossoms flame,
    And the bracken is bronzing to
    brown.
With the turf 'neath our tread and the blue
    overhead,
    And the song of the lark in the
    whin ;
There 's the flag and the green, with the
    bunkers between —
    Now will you be over or in ?

The doctor may come, and we 'll teach
    him to know
A tee where no tannin can lurk;
The soldier may come, and we 'll promise
    to show
Some hazards a soldier may shirk;
The statesman may joke, as he tops every
    stroke,
    That at last he is high in his
    aims;
And the clubman will stand with a club
    in his hand
    That is worth every club in St.
    James'.

The palm and the leather come rarely
    together,
Gripping the driver's haft,

And it 's good to feel the jar of the
 steel
 And the spring of the hickory shaft.
Why trouble or seek for the praise of a
 clique —
 A cleek here is common to all;
And the lie that might sting is a very
 small thing
 When compared with the lie of the '
 ball.

Come youth and come age, from the
 study or stage,
 From Bar or from Bench — high and
 low!
A green you must use as a cure for the
 blues —
 You drive them away as you go.

We 're outward bound on a long, long
    round,
  And it 's time to be up and away:
If worry and sorrow come back with the
    morrow,
  At least we 'll be happy to-day.

THE DYING WHIP

It came from gettin' 'eated, that was 'ow
  the thing begun,
And 'ackin' back to kennels from a ninety-
  minute run;
" I guess I 've copped brownchitis," says
  I to brother Jack,
An' then afore I knowed it I was down
  upon my back.

At night there came a sweatin' as left me
  deadly weak,
And my throat was sort of tickly an' it
  'urt me for to speak;

An' then there came an 'ackin' cough as
would n't leave alone,
An' then afore I knowed it I was only
skin and bone.

I never was a 'eavy weight. I scaled at
seven four,
An' rode at eight, or maybe at just a trifle
more;
And now I 'll stake my davy I would n't
scale at five,
And I 'd 'old my own at catch-weights
with the skinniest jock alive.

And the doctor says the reason why I sit
an' cough an' wheeze
Is all along o' varmint, like the cheese-
mites in the cheese;

The smallest kind o' varmint, but varmint
    all the same,
Microscopes or somethin'— I forget the
    varmint's name.

But I knows as I 'm a goner.   They never
    said as much,
But I reads the people's faces, and I knows
    as I am such;
Well, there 's 'Urst to mind the 'orses and
    the 'ounds can look to Jack,
Though 'e never was a patch on me in
    'andlin' of a pack.

You 'll maybe think I 'm boastin', but
    you 'll find they all agree
That there 's not a whip in Surrey as can
    'andle 'ounds like me;

Fo I knew 'em all from puppies, and I 'd
    tell 'em without fail —
If I seed a tail a-waggin', I could tell
    who wagged the tail.

And voices — why, Lor' love you, it 's
    more than I can 'elp,
It just comes kind of natural to know
    each whine an' yelp;
You might take them twenty couple where
    you will and let 'em run,
An' I 'd listen by the coverside and name
    'em one by one.

I say it 's kind of natural, for since I was
    a brat
I never cared for readin' books, or fancy
    things like that;

But give me 'ounds and 'orses an' I was
    quite content,
An' I loved to 'ear 'em talkin' and to won-
    der what they meant.

And when the 'ydrophoby came five year
    ago next May,
When Nailer was be'avin' in a most ow-
    dacious way,
I fixed him so 's 'e could n't bite, my
    'ands on neck an' back,
An' I 'eaved 'im from the kennels, and
    they say I saved the pack.

An' when the Master 'eard of it, 'e up an'
    says, says 'e,
" If that chap were a soldier man, they 'd
    give him the V. C."

Which is some kind o' medal what they
  give to soldier men;
An' Master said if I were such I would 'a'
  got it then.

Parson brought 'is Bible and come to read
  to me;
"'Ave what you like, there 's everythink
  within this Book," says 'e.
Says I, " They 've left the 'orses out!"
  Says 'e, " You are mistook ";
An' 'e up an' read a 'eap of things about
  them from the Book.

And some of it amazin' fine; although
  I 'm fit to swear
No 'orse would ever say " Ah, ah!" same
  as they said it there.

Per'aps it was an 'Ebrew 'orse the chap
 'ad in his mind,
But I never 'eard an English 'orse say
 nothin' of the kind.

Parson is a good 'un. I 've known 'im
 from a lad;
'T was me as taught 'im ridin', an' 'e
 rides uncommon bad;
And he says—— But 'ark an' listen!
 There 's an 'orn! I 'eard it blow;
Pull the blind from off the winder! Prop
 me up, and 'old me so.

They 're 'rawing the black 'anger, just
 aside the Squire's grounds.
'Ark and listen! 'Ark and listen! There 's
 the yappin' of the 'ounds:

There 's Fanny and Beltinker, and I 'ear
  old Boxer call;
You see I was n't boastin' when I said I
  knew 'em all.

Let me sit an' 'old the bed-rail! Now I
  see 'em as they pass:
There 's Squire upon the Midland mare,
  . a good 'un on the grass;
But this is closish country, and you wants
  a clever 'orse
When 'alf the time you 're in the woods
  an' 'alf among the gorse.

'Ark to Jack a-'ollering—a-bleatin' like a
  lamb.
You would n't think it now, perhaps, to
  see the thing I am;

But there was a time the ladies used to
    linger at the meet
Just to 'ear me callin' in the woods: my
    callin' was so sweet.

I see the cross-roads corner, with the field
    awaitin' there,
There 's Purcell on 'is piebald 'orse, an'
    doctor on the mare,
And the Master on 'is iron gray; she is n't
    much to look,
But I seed 'er do clean twenty foot across
    the 'eathly brook.

There 's Captain Kane an' McIntyre an'
    'alf a dozen more,
And two or three are 'untin' whom I
    never seed afore;

Likely-lookin' chaps they be, well groomed
    and 'orsed and dressed —
I wish they could 'a' seen the pack when
    it was at its best.

It 's a check, and they are drawing down
    the coppice for a scent,
You can see as they 've been runnin', for
    the 'orses they are spent;
I 'll lay the fox will break this way, down-
    wind as sure as fate,
An' if he does you 'll see the field come
    poundin' through our gate.

But, Maggie, what 's that slinkin' beside
    the cover? — See!
Now it 's in the clover field, and goin'
    fast an' free,

It 's 'im, and they don't see 'im.   It 's
    'im!   'Alloo! 'Alloo!
My broken wind won't run to it — I 'll
    leave the job to you.

There, now I 'ear the music, and I know
    they 're on his track;
Oh, watch 'em, Maggie, watch 'em!   Ain't
    they just a lovely pack!
I 've nursed 'em through distemper, an'
    I 've trained an' broke 'em in,
An' my 'eart it just goes out to them as if
    they was my kin.

Well, all things 'as an endin', as I 've
    'eard the parson say,
The 'orse is cast, an' the 'ound is past, an'
    the 'unter 'as 'is day;

But my day was yesterday, so lay me
down again.
You can draw the curtain, Maggie, right
across the window-pane.

MASTER

Master went a-hunting,
  When the leaves were falling;
We saw him on the bridle path,
  We heard him gaily calling.
"Oh, master, master, come you back,
For I have dreamed a dream so black!"
  A glint of steel from bit and heel,
  The chestnut cantered faster,
A red flash seen amid the green,
  And so good-by to master.

Master came from hunting,
  Two silent comrades bore him;
His eyes were dim, his face was white,
  The mare was led before him.

"Oh, master, master, is it thus
That you have come again to us?"
   I held my lady's ice-cold hand,
      They bore the hurdle past her;
   Why should they go so soft and slow?
   It matters not to master.

H. M. S. "FOUDROYANT"

[*Being an humble address to Her Majesty's Naval advisers, who sold Nelson's old flagship to the Germans for a thousand pounds.*]

Who says the Nation's purse is lean,
    Who fears for claim or bond or debt,
When all the glories that have been
    Are scheduled as a cash asset?
If times are black and trade is slack,
    If coal and cotton fail at last,
We 've something left to barter yet —
    Our glorious past.

There 's many a crypt in which lies hid
    The dust of statesman or of king;

There 's Shakespeare's home to raise a bid,
  And Milton's house its price would
    bring.
What for the sword that Cromwell drew?
  What for Prince Edward's coat of mail?
What for our Saxon Alfred's tomb?
    They 're all for sale!

And stone and marble may be sold
  Which serve no present daily need;
There 's Edward's Windsor, labeled old,
  And Wolsey's palace, guaranteed.
St. Clement Danes and fifty fanes,
  The Tower and the Temple grounds;
How much for these?   Just price them,
    please,
      In British pounds.

You hucksters, have you still to learn
  The things which money will not buy?

Can you not read that, cold and stern
   As we may be, there still does lie
Deep in our hearts a hungry love
   For what concerns our island story?
We sell our work — perchance our lives,
      But not our glory.

Go barter to the knacker's yard
   The steed that has outlived its time!
Send hungry to the pauper ward
   The man who served you in his prime!
But when you touch the Nation's store,
   Be broad your mind and tight your grip.
Take heed!   And bring us back once
     more
     Our Nelson's ship.

And if no mooring can be found
   In all our harbors near or far,

Then tow the old three-decker round
  To where the deep-sea soundings are;
There, with her pennon flying clear,
  And with her ensign lashed peak high,
Sink her a thousand fathoms sheer.
    There let her lie!

THE FARNSHIRE CUP

Christopher Davis was up upon Mavis
    And Sammy MacGregor on Flo,
Jo Chauncy rode Spider, the rankest out-
    sider,
    But *he 'd* make a wooden horse go.
There was Robin and Leah and Boadicea,
    And Chesterfield's Son of the Sea;
And Irish Nuneaton, who never was
    beaten,
    They backed her at seven to three.

The course was the devil! A start on the
    level,
    And then a stiff breather uphill;
A bank at the top with a four-foot drop,
    And a bullfinch down by the mill.

A stretch of straight from the Whittlesea
    gate,
  Then up and down and up;
And the mounts that stay through Farn-
    shire clay
  May bid for the Farnshire Cup.

The tipsters were touting, the bookies
    were shouting
  " Bar one, bar one, bar one!"
With a glint and a glimmer of silken
    shimmer
  The field shone bright in the sun,
When Farmer Brown came riding down:
  " I hain't much time to spare,
But I 've entered her name, so I 'll play
    out the game,
  On the back o' my old gray mare.

" You never would think 'er a thorough-
    bred clinker,
    There 's never a judge that would;
Each leg be'ind 'as a splint, you 'll find,
    And the fore are none too good.
She roars a bit, and she don't look fit,
    She 's molted 'alf 'er 'air;
But——" He smiled in a way that
    seemed to say
    That he knew that old gray mare.

And the bookies laughed and the bookies
    chaffed,
    " Who backs the mare ? " cried they.
" A hundred to one! " " It 's done — and
    done ! "
    " We 'll take that price all day."
" What if the mare is shedding hair !
    What if her eye is wild !

We read her worth and her pedigree birth
    In the smile that her owner smiled."

And the whisper grew and the whisper
    flew
    That she came of Isonomy stock.
" Fifty to one ! " " It 's done — and done !
    Look at her haunch and hock !
Ill-groomed ! Why, yes, but one may
    guess
    That that is her owner's guile."
Ah, Farmer Brown, the sharps from town
    Have read your simple smile !

They 've weighed him in. " Now lose or
    win,
    I 've money at stake this day ;
Gee-long, my sweet, and if we 're beat,
    We 'll both do all we may ! "

He joins the rest, they line abreast,
    "Back Leah! Mavis up!"
The flag is dipped and the field is slipped,
    Full split for the Farnshire Cup.

Christopher Davis is leading on Mavis,
    Spider is waiting on Flo;
Boadicea is gaining on Leah,
    Irish Nuneaton lies low;
Robin is tailing, his wind has been failing,
    Son of the Sea 's going fast:
So crack on the pace, for it 's any one's
    race,
    And the winner 's the horse that can
    last.

Chestnut and bay, and sorrel and gray,
    See how they glimmer and gleam!

Bending and straining, and losing and
 gaining,
 Silk jackets flutter and stream;
They are over the grass as the cloud
 shadows pass,
 They are up to the fence at the top;
It 's " hey then!" and over, and into the
 clover,
 There was n't one slip at the drop.

They are all going still: they are round
 by the mill,
 They are down by the Whittlesea
 gate;
Leah 's complaining, and Mavis is
 gaining,
 And Flo 's catching up in the
 straight.

Robin's gone wrong, but the Spider runs
    strong,
    He sticks to the leader like wax;
An utter outsider, but look at his rider —
    Jo Chauncy, the pick of the cracks!

Robin was tailing and pecked at a paling,
    Leah's gone weak in her feet;
Boadicea came down at the railing,
    Son of the Sea is dead beat.
Leather to leather, they're pounding
    together,
    Three of them all in a row;
And Irish Nuneaton, who never was beaten,
    Is level with Spider and Flo.

It's into the straight from the Whittlesea
    gate,
    Clean galloping over the green,

But four foot high the hurdles lie
  With a sunken ditch between.
'T is a bit of a test for a beast at its best,
  And the devil and all at its worst;
But it 's clear run in with the Cup to win
  For the horse that is over it first.

So try it, my beauties, and fly it, my
    beauties,
  Spider, Nuneaton, and Flo;
With a trip and a blunder there 's one
    of them under,
  Hark to it crashing below!
Is it the brown or the sorrel that 's down?
  It 's the brown! It is Flo who is in!
And Spider with Chauncy, the pick of the
    fancy,
  Is going full split for a win.

"Spider is winning!" "Jo Chauncy is
    winning!"
    "He 's winning! He 's winning!
    Bravo!"
The bookies are raving, the ladies are
    waving,
    The Stand is all shouting for Jo.
The horse is clean done, but the race may
    be won
    By the Newmarket lad on his
    back ;
For the fire of the rider may bring an out-
    sider
    Ahead of a thoroughbred crack.

"Spider is winning!" "Jo Chauncy is
    winning!"
    It swells like the roar of the sea;

But Jo hears the drumming of somebody
    coming,
And sees a lean head by his knee.
"Nuneaton! Nuneaton! The Spider is
    beaten!"
It is but a spurt at the most;
For lose it or win it, they have but a
    minute
Before they are up with the post.

Nuneaton is straining, Nuneaton is gain-
    ing,
Neither will falter nor flinch;
Whips they are plying and jackets are
    flying,
They 're fairly abreast to an inch.
"Crack 'em up! Let 'em go! Well
    ridden! Bravo!"
Gamer ones never were bred;

" Jo Chauncy has done it!   He 's spurted!
   He 's won it!"
   The favorite 's beat by a head!

Don't tell me of luck, for it 's judgment
      and pluck
   And a courage that never will shirk;
To give your mind to it and know how
      to do it
   And put all your heart in your work.
So here 's to the Spider, the winning out-
      sider,
   With little Jo Chauncy up;
May they stay life's course, both jockey
      and horse,
   As they stayed in the Farnshire Cup.

But it 's possible that you are wondering
      what
   May have happened to Farmer Brown,

And the old gray crock of Isonomy stock
  Who was backed by the sharps from
    town.
She blew and she sneezed, she coughed
    and she wheezed,
  She ran till her knees gave way;
But never a grumble at trip or at stumble
  Was heard from her jock that day.

For somebody laid *against* the gray,
  And somebody made a pile;
And Brown says he can make farming pay,
  And he smiles a simple smile.
" Them sharps from town were riled," says
    Brown;
  " But I can't see why — can you ?
For I said quite fair as I knew that mare,
  And I proved my words was true."

THE GROOM'S STORY

Ten mile in twenty minutes! 'E done it,
    sir.   That 's true.
The big bay 'orse in the further stall —
    the one wot 's next to you.
I 've seen some better 'orses; I 've seldom
    seen a wuss,
But 'e 'olds the bloomin' record, an' that 's
    good enough for us.

We knew as it was in 'im. 'E 's thorough-
    bred, three part,
We bought 'im for to race 'im, but we
    found 'e 'ad no 'eart;

For 'e was sad and thoughtful, and amazin'
  dignified,
It seemed a kind o' liberty to drive 'im or
  to ride;

For 'e never seemed a-thinkin' of what 'e
  'ad to do,
But 'is thoughts was set on 'igher things,
  admirin' of the view.
'E looked a puffeck pictur, and a pictur
  'e would stay,
'E would n't even switch 'is tail to drive
  the flies away.

And yet we knew 't was in 'im; we knew
  as 'e could fly;
But what we could n't git at was 'ow to
  make 'im try.

We 'd almost turned the job up, until at
    last one day
We got the last yard out of 'im in a most
    amazin' way.

It was all along o' master; which master
    'as the name
Of a reg'lar true blue sportman, an' al-
    ways acts the same;
But we all 'as weaker moments, which
    master 'e 'ad one,
An' 'e went and bought a motor-car when
    motor-cars begun.

I seed it in the stable yard — it fairly
    turned me sick —
A greasy, wheezy engine as can neither
    buck or kick.

You 've a screw to drive it forrard, and a
    screw to make it stop,
For it was foaled in a smithy stove an'
    bred in a blacksmith shop.

It did n't want no stable, it didn't ask no
    groom,
It did n't need no nothin' but a bit o'
    standin' room.
Just fill it up with paraffin an' it would go
    all day,
Which the same should be agin the law
    if I could 'ave my way.

Well, master took 'is motor-car, an' moted
    'ere an' there,
A frightenin' the 'orses an' a poisonin' the
    air.

'E wore a bloomin' yachtin' cap, but Lor'!
  wot *did* 'e know,
Excep' that if you turn a screw the thing
  would stop or go?

An' then one day it would n't go. 'E
  screwed and screwed again,
But somethin' jammed, an' there 'e stuck
  in the mud of a country lane.
It 'urt 'is pride most cruel, but what was
  'e to do?
So at last 'e bade me fetch a 'orse to pull
  the motor through.

This was the 'orse we fetched 'im; an'
  when we reached the car,
We braced 'im tight and proper to the
  middle of the bar,

And buckled up 'is traces and lashed them
    to each side,
While 'e 'eld 'is 'ead so 'aughtily, an'
    looked most dignified.

Not bad tempered, mind you, but kind
    of pained and vexed,
And 'e seemed to say, " Well, bli' me !
    wot *will* they ask me next ?
I 've put up with some liberties, but this
    caps all by far,
To be assistant engine to a crocky motor-
    car ! "

Well, master 'e was in the car, a-fiddlin'
    with the gear,
And the 'orse was meditatin', an' I was
    standin' near,

When master 'e touched somethin'—
    what it was we'll never know —
But it sort o' spurred the boiler up and
    made the engine go.

"'Old 'ard, old gal!" says master, and
    "Gently then!" says I,
But an engine won't 'eed coaxin' an' it
    ain't no use to try;
So first 'e pulled a lever, an' then 'e turned
    a screw,
But the thing kept crawlin' forrard spite
    of all that 'e could do.

And first he went quite slowly and the
    'orse went also slow,
But 'e 'ad to buck up faster when the
    wheels began to go;

For the car kept crowdin' on 'im and but-
    tin' 'im along,
And in less than 'alf a minute, sir, that
    'orse was goin' strong.

At first 'e walked quite dignified, an' then
    'e 'ad to trot,
And then 'e tried a canter when the pace
    became too 'ot.
'E looked 'is very 'aughtiest, as if 'e did n't
    mind,
And all the time the motor-car was push-
    in' 'im be'ind.

Now, master lost 'is 'ead when 'e found 'e
    could n't stop,
And 'e pulled a valve or somethin' an'
    somethin' else went pop,

An' somethin' else went fizzywiz, and in
    a flash, or less,
That blessed car was goin' like a limited
    express.

Master 'eld the steerin' gear, an' kept the
    road all right,
And away they whizzed and clattered —
    my aunt! it was a sight.
'E seemed the finest draught 'orse as ever
    lived by far,
For all the country Juggins thought 't was
    'im wot pulled the car.

'E was stretchin' like a gray'ound, 'e was
    goin' all 'e knew;
But it bumped an' shoved be'ind 'im, for
    all that 'e could do;

It butted 'im an' boosted 'im an' spanked
    'im on a'ead,
Till 'e broke the ten-mile record, same as
    I already said.

Ten mile in twenty minutes! 'E done it,
    sir.   That 's true.
The only time we ever found what that
    'ere 'orse could do.
Some say it was n't 'ardly fair, and the
    papers made a fuss,
But 'e broke the ten-mile record, and
    that 's good enough for us.

You see that 'orse's tail, sir? You don't!
    No more do we,
Which really ain't surprisin', for 'e 'as no
    tail to see;

That engine wore it off 'im before master
    made it stop,
And all the road was littered like a
    bloomin' barber's shop.

And master? Well, it cured 'im. 'E
    altered from that day,
And come back to 'is 'orses in the good
    old-fashioned way.
And if you wants to git the sack, the
    quickest way by far
Is to 'int as 'ow you think 'e ought to
    keep a motor-car.

WITH THE CHIDDINGFOLDS

The horse is bedded down
　　Where the straw lies deep.
The hound is in the kennel;
　　Let the poor hound sleep!
And the fox is in the spinney
　　By the run which he is haunting,
And I 'll lay an even guinea
　　That a goose or two is wanting
When the farmer comes to count them in
　　the morning.

The horse is up and saddled;
　　Girth the old horse tight!
The hounds are out and drawing
　　In the morning light.

Now it's "Yoick!" among the heather,
And it's "Yoick!" across the clover,
And it 's " To him, altogether ! "
" Hyke a Bertha ! Hyke a Rover !"
And the woodlands smell so sweetly in
the morning.

" There 's Termagant a-whimper-
ing ;
She whimpers so."
"There 's a young hound yapping!"
Let the young hound go !
But the old hound is cunning,
And it 's him we mean to follow,
" They are running ! They are run-
ning ! "
And it 's " Forrard to the hollo !"
For the scent is lying strongly in the
morning.

" Who 's the fool that heads him ? "
    Hold hard, and let him pass !
He 's out among the oziers,
    He 's clear upon the grass.
You grip his flanks and settle,
    For the horse is stretched and
        straining,
Here 's a game to test your mettle,
    And a sport to try your training,
When the Chiddingfolds are running in
        the morning.

We 're up by the Coppice
    And we 're down by the Mill,
We 're out upon the Common,
    And the hounds are running still.
You must tighten on the leather,
    For we blunder through the
        bracken ;

Though you 're over hocks in heather
Still the pace must never slacken
As we race through Thursley Common in
the morning.

We are breaking from the tangle,
We are out upon the green,
There 's a bank and a hurdle
With a quickset between.
You must steady him and try it,
You are over with a scramble.
Here 's a wattle! You must fly it,
And you land among the bramble,
For it 's roughish, toughish going in the
morning.

'Ware the bog by the Grove
As you pound through the slush.
See the whip! See the huntsman!
We are close upon his brush.

'Ware the root that lies before you!
It will trip you if you blunder.
'Ware the branch that 's drooping
o'er you!
You must dip and swerve from
under
As you gallop through the woodland in
the morning

There were fifty at the find,
There were forty at the mill,
There were twenty on the heath,
And ten are going still.
Some are pounded, some are shirking,
And they dwindle and diminish
Till a weary pair are working,
Spent and blowing, to the finish,
And we hear the shrill whoo-ooping in the
morning.

The horse is bedded down
　　Where the straw lies deep,
The hound is in the kennel,
　　He is yapping in his sleep.
But the fox is in the spinney
　　Lying snug in earth and burrow.
And I 'll lay an even guinea
　　We could find again to-morrow,
If we chose to go a-hunting in the morning.

A HUNTING MORNING

Put the saddle on the mare,
    For the wet winds blow;
There's winter in the air,
    And autumn all below.
For the red leaves are flying
And the red bracken dying,
And the red fox lying
    Where the oziers grow.

Put the bridle on the mare,
    For my blood runs chill;
And my heart, it is there,
    On the heather-tufted hill,

With the gray skies o'er us,
And the long-drawn chorus
Of a running pack before us
　　From the find to the kill.

Then lead round the mare,
　　For it 's time that we began,
And away with thought and care,
　　Save to live and be a man,
While the keen air is blowing,
And the huntsman holloing,
And the black mare going
　　As the black mare can.

THE OLD GRAY FOX

We started from the Valley Pride,
  And Farnham way we went.
We waited at the cover-side,
  But never found a scent.
Then we tried the withy beds
  Which grow by Frensham town,
And there we found the old gray fox,
    The same old fox,
    The game old fox;
Yes, there we found the old gray fox,
  Which lives on Hankley Down.
        So here 's to the master,
        And here 's to the man!
        And here 's to twenty couple
        Of the white and black and tan!

Here 's a find without a wait!
Here 's a hedge without a gate!
Here 's the man who follows straight,
Where the old fox ran.

The Member rode his thoroughbred,
Doctor had the gray,
The Soldier led on a roan red,
The Sailor rode the bay.
Squire was there on his Irish mare,
And Parson on the brown;
And so we chased the old gray fox,
The same old fox,
The game old fox;
And so we chased the old gray fox
Across the Hankley Down.
So here 's to the master,
And here 's to the man!
&c.   &c.   &c.

The Doctor's gray was going strong
   Until she slipped and fell;
He had to keep his bed so long
   His patients all got well.
The Member he had lost his seat,
   'T was carried by his horse;
And so we chased the old gray fox,
     The same old fox,
     The game old fox;
And so we chased the old gray fox
   That earthed in Hankley Gorse.
        So here 's to the master,
        And here 's to the man!
        &c.   &c.   &c.

The Parson sadly fell away,
   And in the furze did lie;
The words we heard that Parson say
   Made all the horses shy!

The Sailor he was seen no more
  Upon that stormy bay;
But still we chased the old gray fox,
    The same old fox,
    The game old fox;
Still we chased the old gray fox
  Through all the winter day.
        So here 's to the master,
        And here 's to the man!
        &c.   &c.   &c.

And when we found him gone to ground,
  They sent for spade and man ;
But Squire said "Shame! The beast was
    game!
  A gamer never ran!"
His wind and pace have gained the race,
  His life is fairly won.

But may we meet the old gray fox,
  The same old fox,
  The game old fox;
May we meet the old gray fox
  Before the year is done.
      So here 's to the master,
      And here 's to the man!
    And here 's to twenty couple
    Of the white and black and tan!
    Here 's a find without a wait!
    Here 's a hedge without a gate!
    Here 's the man who follows straight,
      Where the old fox ran.

'WARE HOLES

['*Ware Holes!* is the expression used in the hunting-field to warn those behind against rabbit-burrows or other such dangers.]

A sportin' death! My word it was!
An' taken in a sportin' way.
Mind you, I was n't there to see;
I only tell you what they say.

They found that day at Shillinglee,
An' ran 'im down to Chillinghurst;
The fox was goin' straight an' free
For ninety minutes at a burst.

They 'ad a check at Ebernoe
　An' made a cast across the Down,
Until they got a view 'ollo
　An' chased 'im up to Kirdford town.

From Kirdford 'e run Bramber way,
　An' took 'em over 'arf the Weald.
If you 'ave tried the Sussex clay,
　You 'll guess it weeded out the field.

Until at last I don't suppose
　As 'arf a dozen, at the most,
Came safe to where the grassland goes
　Switchbackin' southwards to the coast.

Young Captain 'Eadley, 'e was there,
　And Jim the whip an' Percy Day;
The Purcells an' Sir Charles Adair,
　An' this 'ere gent from London way.

For 'e 'ad gone amazin' fine,
    Two 'undred pounds between 'is
        knees;
Eight stone he was, an' rode at nine,
    As light an' limber as you please.

'E was a stranger to the 'Unt,
    There were n't a person as 'e knew
        there;
But 'e could ride, that London gent—
    'E sat 'is mare as if 'e grew there.

They seed the 'ounds upon the scent,
    But found a fence across their track,
And 'ad to fly it; else it meant
    A turnin' and a 'arkin' back.

'E was the foremost at the fence,
    And as 'is mare just cleared the rail

He turned to them that rode be'ind,
  For three was at 'is very tail.

" 'Ware 'oles!" says 'e, an' with the word,
  Still sittin' easy on his mare,
Down, down 'e went, an' down an' down,
  Into the quarry yawnin' there.

Some say it was two 'undred foot;
  The bottom lay as black as ink.
I guess they 'ad some ugly dreams,
  Who reined their 'orses on the brink.

'E 'd only time for that one cry;
  " 'Ware 'oles!" says 'e, an' saves all
    three. .
There may be better deaths to die,
  But that one 's good enough for me.

For mind you, 't was a sportin' end,
    Upon a right good sportin' day;
They think a deal of 'im down 'ere,
    That gent what came from London
way.

THE HOME-COMING OF THE "EURYDICE"

[Lost, with her crew of three hundred boys, on the last day of her voyage, March 23, 1876. She foundered off Portsmouth, from which town many of the boys came.]

Up with the royals that top the white
    spread of her!
Press her and dress her, and drive
    through the foam;
The Island 's to port, and the mainland
    ahead of her,
    Hey for the Warner and Hayling and
    Home!

" Bo'sun, O Bo'sun, just look at the green
    of it!
Look at the red cattle down by the hedge!

Look at the farmsteading — all that is
 seen of it,
 One little gable end over the edge!"

"Lord! the tongues of them clattering,
 clattering,
 All growing wild at a peep of the
  Wight;
Aye, sir, aye, it has set them all chattering,
 Thinking of home and their mothers
  to-night."

Spread the topgallants — oh, lay them out
 lustily!
 What though it darken o'er Netherby
  Combe?
'T is but the valley wind, puffing so
 gustily —
 On for the Warner and Hayling and
  Home!

" Bo'sun, O Bo'sun, just see the long slope
    of it!
Culver is there, with the cliff and the
    light.
Tell us, oh tell us, now is there a hope of it?
Shall we have leave for our homes for
    to-night ? "

" Tut, the clack of them!   Steadily!
    Steadily!
Aye, as you say, sir, they 're little ones
    still;
One long reach should open it readily,
    Round by St. Helen's and under the hill.

" The Spit and the Nab are the gates of
    the promise,
Their mothers to them — and to us it 's
    our wives.

I 've sailed forty years, and — By God, it 's
    upon us!
Down royals, down tops'ls, down,
    down for your lives!"

A gray swirl of snow with the squall at
    the back of it,
Heeling her, reeling her, beating her
    down!
A gleam of her bends in the thick of the
    wrack of it,
A flutter of white in the eddies of
    brown.

It broke in one moment of blizzard and
    blindness;
The next, like a foul bat, it flapped on
    its way.

But our ship and our boys!   Gracious
    Lord, in your kindness,
Give help to the mothers who need it
    to-day !

Give help to the women who wait by the
    water,
Who stand on the Hard with their eyes
    past the Wight.
Ah ! whisper it gently, you sister or
    daughter,
" Our boys are all gathered at home for
    to-night."

THE INNER ROOM

It is mine —the little chamber,
    Mine alone.
I had it from my forebears
    Years agone.
Yet within its walls I see
A most motley company,
And they one and all claim me
    As their own.

There 's one who is a soldier
    Bluff and keen ;
Single-minded, heavy-fisted,
    Rude of mien.

He would gain a purse or stake it,
He would win a heart or break it,
He would give a life or take it,
    Conscience-clean.

And near him is a priest
    Still schism-whole ;
He loves the censer-reek
    And organ-roll.
He has leanings to the mystic,
Sacramental, eucharistic ;
And dim yearnings altruistic
    Thrill his soul.

There 's another who with doubts
    Is overcast ;
I think him younger brother
    To the last.

Walking wary stride by stride,
Peering forwards anxious-eyed,
Since he learned to doubt his guide
    In the past.

And 'mid them all, alert,
    But somewhat cowed,
There sits a stark-faced fellow,
    Beetle-browed,
Whose black soul shrinks away
From a lawyer-ridden day,
And has thoughts he dare not say
    Half avowed.

There are others who are sitting,
    Grim as doom,
In the dim ill-boding shadow
    Of my room.

Darkling figures, stern or quaint,
Now a savage, now a saint,
Showing fitfully and faint
    Through the gloom.

And those shadows are so dense,
    There may be
Many — very many — more
    Than I see.
They are sitting day and night,
Soldier, rogue, and anchorite;
And they wrangle and they fight
    Over me.

If the stark-faced fellow win,
    All is o'er!
If the priest should gain his will,
    I doubt no more!

But if each shall have his day,
I shall swing and I shall sway
In the same old weary way
   As before.

THE IRISH COLONEL

Said the king to the colonel,
" The complaints are eternal,
   That you Irish give more trouble
   Than any other corps."

Said the colonel to the king,
" This complaint is no new thing,
   For your foemen, sire, have made it
   A hundred times before."

THE BLIND ARCHER

Little boy Love drew his bow at a chance,
  Shooting down at the ballroom floor;
He hit an old chaperon watching the
    dance,
  And oh! but he wounded her sore.
    " Hey, Love, you could n't mean
      that!
    Hi, Love, what would you be at?"
      No word would he say,
      But he flew on his way,
For the little boy's busy, and how could
    he stay?

Little boy Love drew a shaft just for sport
  At the soberest club in Pall Mall;

He winged an old veteran drinking his port,
And down that old veteran fell.
 "Hey, Love, you must n't do that!
 Hi, Love, what would you be at?
  This cannot be right!
  It 's ludicrous quite!"
But it 's no use to argue, for Love 's out of
 sight.

A sad-faced young clerk in a cell all apart
Was planning a celibate vow;
But the boy's random arrow has sunk in
 his heart,
And the cell is an empty one now.
 "Hey, Love, you must n't do that!
 Hi, Love, what would you be at?
  He is not for you,
  He has duties to do."
"But I *am* his duty," quoth Love as he flew.

The king sought a bride, and the nation
    had hoped
    For a queen without rival or peer.
But the little boy shot, and the king has
    eloped
    With Miss No-one on nothing a year.
      " Hey, love, you could n't mean that !
      Hi, Love, what would you be at ?
        What an impudent thing
        To make game of a king !"
" But *I'm* a king also," cried Love on the
    wing.

Little boy Love grew pettish one day;
    " If you keep on complaining," he
      swore,
" I 'll pack both my bow and my quiver
      away,
    And so I shall plague you no more."

"Hey, Love, you must n't do that!
Hi, Love, what would you be at?
You may ruin our ease,
You may do what you please,
But we can't do without you, you sweet
little tease!"

A PARABLE

The cheese-mites asked how the cheese
 got there,
And warmly debated the matter;
The Orthodox said that it came from the
 air,
And the heretics said from the platter.
They argued it long and they argued it
 strong,
And I hear they are arguing now;
But of all the choice spirits who lived in
 the cheese,
Not one of them thought of a cow.

A TRAGEDY

Who 's that walking on the moorland?
 Who 's that moving on the hill?
They are passing 'mid the bracken,
But the shadows grow and blacken,
  And I cannot see them clearly on
  the hill.

Who 's that calling on the moorland?
 Who 's that crying on the hill?
Was it bird or was it human,
Was it child, or man, or woman,
  Who was calling so sadly on the hill?

Who 's that running on the moorland?
    Who 's that flying on the hill?
He is there — and there again,
But you cannot see him plain,
·   For the shadow lies so darkly on the
    hill.

What 's that lying in the heather?
    What 's that lurking on the hill?
My horse will go no nearer,
And I cannot see it clearer,
    But there 's something that is lying
    on the hill.

THE PASSING

It was the hour of dawn,
   When the heart beats thin and small,
The window glimmered gray,
   Framed in a shadow wall.

And in the cold sad light
   Of the early morningtide,
The dear, dead girl came back
   And stood by his bedside.

The girl he lost came back;
   He saw her flowing hair;
It flickered and it waved
   Like a breath in frosty air.

As in a steamy glass,
  Her face was dim and blurred;
Her voice was sweet and thin,
  Like the calling of a bird.

" You said that you would come,
  You promised not to stay;
And I have waited here,
  To help you on the way.

" I have waited on,
  But still you bide below;
You said that you would come,
  And oh, I want you so!

" For half my soul is here,
  And half my soul is there,
When you are on the earth
  And I am in the air.

" But on your dressing-stand
    There lies a triple key;
Unlock the little gate
    Which fences you from me.

" Just one little pang,
    Just one throb of pain,
And then your weary head
    Between my breasts again."

In the dim unhomely light
    Of the early morningtide,
He took the triple key
    And he laid it by his side.

A pistol, silver chased,
    An open hunting-knife,
A phial of the drug
    Which cures the ill of life.

He looked upon the three,
    And sharply drew his breath :
" Now help me, oh my love,
    For I fear this cold gray death."

She bent her face above,
    She kissed him and she smiled;
She soothed him as a mother
    May soothe a frightened child.

" Just that little pang, love,
    Just a throb of pain,
And then your weary head
    Between my breasts again."

He snatched the pistol up,
    He pressed it to his ear;
But a sudden sound broke in,
    And his skin was raw with fear.

He took the hunting-knife,
  He tried to raise the blade;
It glimmered cold and white,
  And he was sore afraid.

He poured the potion out,
  But it was thick and brown;
His throat was sealed against it,
  And he could not drain it down.

He looked to her for help,
  And when he looked — behold!
His love was there before him
  As in the days of old.

He saw the drooping head,
  He saw the gentle eyes;
He saw the same shy grace of hers
  He had been wont to prize.

She pointed and she smiled,
And lo! he was aware
Of a half-lit bedroom chamber
And a silent figure there.

A silent figure lying,
A-sprawl upon a bed;
With a silver-mounted pistol
Still clotted to his head.

And as he downward gazed,
Her voice came full and clear,
The homely tender voice
Which he had loved to hear:

" The key is very certain,
The door is sealed to none.
You did it, oh, my darling!
And you never knew it done.

" When the net was broken,
    You thought you felt its mesh;
You carried to the spirit
    The troubles of the flesh.

" And are you trembling still, dear?
    Then let me take your hand;
And I will lead you outward
    To a sweet and restful land.

" You know how once in London
    I put my griefs on you;
But I can carry yours now —
    Most sweet it is to do!

" Most sweet it is to do, love,
    And very sweet to plan
How I, the helpless woman,
    Can help the helpful man.

" But let me see you smiling
  With the smile I know so well;
Forget the world of shadows,
  And the empty broken shell.

" It is the worn-out garment
  In which you tore a rent;
You tossed it down, and carelessly
  Upon your way you went.

" It is not *you*, my sweetheart,
  For you are here with me.
That frame was but the promise of
  The thing that was to be —

" A tuning of the choir
  Ere the harmonies begin;
And yet it is the image
  Of the subtle thing within.

" There 's not a trick of body,
    There 's not a trait of mind,
But you bring it over with you,
    Ethereal, refined,

' But still the same; for surely
    If we altered as we die,
You would be you no longer,
    And I would not be I.

" I might be an angel,
    But not the girl you knew;
You might be immaculate,
    But that would not be you.

" And now I see you smiling,
    So, darling, take my hand;
And I will lead you outward
    To a sweet and pleasant land.

" Where thought is clear and nimble,
　　Where life is pure and fresh,
Where the soul comes back rejoicing
　　From the mud-bath of the flesh.

"But still the soul is human,
　　With human ways, and so
I love my love in spirit,
　　As I loved him long ago."

So with hands together
　　And fingers twining tight,
The two dead lovers drifted
　　In the golden morning light.

But a gray-haired man was lying
　　Beneath them on a bed,
With a silver-mounted pistol
　　Still clotted to his head.

THE FRANKLIN'S MAID

The franklin he hath gone to roam,
The franklin's maid she bides at home;
But she is cold, and coy, and staid, '
And who may win the franklin's maid?

There came a knight of high renown
In bassinet and ciclatoun;
On bended knee full long he prayed —
He might not win the franklin's maid.

There came a squire so debonair,
His dress was rich, his words were fair.
He sweetly sang, he deftly played —
He could not win the franklin's maid.

There came a mercer wonder-fine,
With velvet cap and gaberdine;
For all his ships, for all his trade,
He could not buy the franklin's maid.

There came an archer bold and true,
With bracer guard and stave of yew;
His purse was light, his jerkin frayed —
Haro, alas! the franklin's maid!

Oh, some have laughed and some have
    cried,
And some have scoured the countryside;
But off they ride through wood and glade,
The bowman and the franklin's maid.

THE OLD HUNTSMAN

There 's a keen and grim old huntsman
　　On a horse as white as snow;
Sometimes he is very swift
　　And sometimes he is slow.
But he never is at fault,
　　For he always hunts at view,
And he rides without a halt
　　　　After you.

The huntsman's name is Death,
　　His horse's name is Time;
He is coming, he is coming,
　　As I sit and write this rhyme;

He is coming, he is coming,
      As you read the rhyme I write;
You can hear the hoofs' low drumming
      Day and night.

You can hear the distant drumming
      As the clock goes tick-a-tack,
And the chiming of the hours
      Is the music of his pack.
You may hardly note their growling
      Underneath the noonday sun,
But at night you hear them howling
      As they run.

And they never check or falter
      For they never miss their kill;
Seasons change and systems alter,
      But the hunt is running still.

Hark! the evening chime is playing,
  O'er the long gray town it peals;
Don't you hear the death-hound baying
  At your heels?

Where is there an earth or burrow?
  Where a cover left for you?
A year, a week, perhaps to-morrow
  Brings the Huntsman's death halloo.
Day by day he gains upon us,
  And the most that we can claim
Is that when the hounds are on us
  We die game.

And somewhere dwells the Master,
  By whom it was decreed;
He sent the savage huntsman,
  He bred the snow-white steed.

These hounds which run forever,
    He set them on your track;
He hears you scream, but never
    Calls them back.

He does not heed our suing,
    We never see his face;
He hunts to our undoing,
    We thank him for the chase.
We thank him and we flatter,
    We hope — because we must —
But have we cause?   No matter!
    Let us trust!